D0734075

June 2008   J.J.
Benton, Lynne
Pirate Pete

DATE DUE

JUN 24 2008	AUG 0 2 2021		
JUL 22 2008			
AUG 0 5 2008			
FEB 2 7 2010			
MAY 1 3 2010			
JUN 0 1 2010			
JUN 2 3 2010			
JUN 2 4 2011			
AUG 0 4 2011			
JUN 1 9 2019			
JUL 0 6 2021			
JUL 0 5 2021			

🐦 Crabtree Publishing Company
www.crabtreebooks.com

PMB16A, 350 Fifth Avenue
Suite 3308,
New York, NY

616 Welland Avenue
St. Catharines, ON
L2M 5V6

Published by Crabtree Publishing in 2008

First published in 2007 by
Franklin Watts
(A division of Hachette Children's Books)
338 Euston Road
London   NW1 3BH

Cataloging-in-Publication data is available at the Library of Congress.

ISBN 978-0-7787-3861-9 (rlb)
ISBN 978-0-7787-3892-3 (pbk)

Series Editor: Jackie Hamley
Editor: Melanie Palmer
Series Advisor: Dr Hilary Minns
Series Designer: Peter Scoulding

Printed in the U.S.A.

Pirate Pete

by Lynne Benton

Illustrated by Neil Chapman

Crabtree Publishing Company

www.crabtreebooks.com

Lynne Benton

"Q: What is green, has two legs, and a chest?

A: A seasick pirate"

Neil Chapman

"When I was a boy, I liked to read about dragons, goblins and pirates. Now it is fun to draw them for my own children to see."

Pete was a pirate.

One day he got
a letter.

It was a map of
a treasure island.

"I must find the treasure!" Pete said.

He sailed to the island.

He climbed up the hill.

He found a treasure
chest ... and opened it.

"Oh!" cried Pirate Pete.

The cake reads: Happy Birthday Pete

Pirate Pete was
very surprised.

They all had
a great party.

"That was even more fun than finding treasure," said Pete.

23

Notes for adults

TADPOLES are structured to provide support for early readers. The stories may also be used by adults for sharing with young children.

Starting to read alone can be daunting. **TADPOLES** help by providing visual support and repeating high frequency words and phrases. These books will both develop confidence and encourage reading and rereading for pleasure.

If you are reading this book with a child, here are a few suggestions:

1. Make reading fun! Choose a time to read when you and the child are relaxed and have time to share the story.
2. Talk about the story before you start reading. Look at the cover and the blurb. What might the story be about? Why might the child like it?
3. Encourage the child to reread the story, and to retell the story in their own words, using the illustrations to remind them what has happened.
4. Discuss the story and see if the child can relate it to their own experiences, or perhaps compare it to another story they know.
5. Give praise! Children learn best in a positive environment.

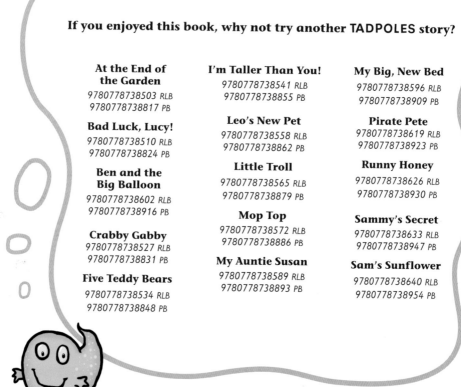

If you enjoyed this book, why not try another TADPOLES story?

At the End of the Garden
9780778738503 *RLB*
9780778738817 *PB*

Bad Luck, Lucy!
9780778738510 *RLB*
9780778738824 *PB*

Ben and the Big Balloon
9780778738602 *RLB*
9780778738916 *PB*

Crabby Gabby
9780778738527 *RLB*
9780778738831 *PB*

Five Teddy Bears
9780778738534 *RLB*
9780778738848 *PB*

I'm Taller Than You!
9780778738541 *RLB*
9780778738855 *PB*

Leo's New Pet
9780778738558 *RLB*
9780778738862 *PB*

Little Troll
9780778738565 *RLB*
9780778738879 *PB*

Mop Top
9780778738572 *RLB*
9780778738886 *PB*

My Auntie Susan
9780778738589 *RLB*
9780778738893 *PB*

My Big, New Bed
9780778738596 *RLB*
9780778738909 *PB*

Pirate Pete
9780778738619 *RLB*
9780778738923 *PB*

Runny Honey
9780778738626 *RLB*
9780778738930 *PB*

Sammy's Secret
9780778738633 *RLB*
9780778738947 *PB*

Sam's Sunflower
9780778738640 *RLB*
9780778738954 *PB*